LAURENCE ANHOLT has created more than 200 books for children which are published throughout the world. His titles have won many awards, such as the Smarties Gold Award on two occasions. His books for Frances Lincoln include the much-loved Chimp and Zee series, *One World Together* and *A Kiss Like This*, created in collaboration with his wife Catherine Anholt, while Laurence is both author and illustrator of the best-selling Anholt's Artists series. The Anholts have three grown-up children and live in a house on a hill above the sea in Devon.

For Claudia, with love.

Find out about all Laurence Anholt's books at www.anholt.co.uk

JANETTA OTTER-BARRY BOOKS

Text and illustrations copyright © Laurence Anholt 2014

First published in Great Britain in 2014 by Frances Lincoln Limited, 74-77 White Lion Street, London N1 9PF
www.franceslincoln.com

This first paperback edition first published in Great Britain in 2015

British Library Cataloguing in Publication Data available on request

ISBN 978-1-84780-658-1

Illustrated with watercolour

Set in Bembo

Printed in China

1 3 5 7 9 8 6 4 2

PHOTOGRAPHIC ACKNOWLEDGEMENTS

Please note: the pages in this book are not numbered. The story begins on page 6.

Paintings by Marc Chagall (1887-1985): Chagall ® / © ADAGP, Paris and DACS, London 2013.

Front cover and page 10 above: *I and the Village* (1911). The Museum of Modern Art, New York. Oil on canvas, 192.1 x 151.4 cm.
Mrs. Simon Guggenheim Fund. 146.1945. Digital image © 2013, The Museum of Modern Art/SCALA, Florence

Page 10 below: *Paris Through the Window* (1913). Solomon R. Guggenheim Museum, New York. Oil on canvas, 136 x 141.9 cm. Photo © 2013,
Art Media/Heritage Images/Scala, Florence

Page 11: *Le Cirque bleu* (1950-52), Detail. Musée National d'Art Moderne – Centre Pompidou, Paris. Oil on canvas, 232 x 175 cm.
Photo © 2013, Scala, Florence

Page 20: *Birthday*, (1915), Detail. The Museum of Modern Art, New York. Oil on cardboard, 80.6 x 99.7 cm. Acquired through the Lillie P. Bliss Bequest.
275.1949. Digital image © 2013, The Museum of Modern Art/SCALA, Florence

Page 21: *Bella and Ida at the Window* (1916), Detail. Private Collection. Oil on canvas, 56.5 x 45 cm. Photo: akg-images

Pages 24-25: *The War* (1964-66). Kunsthaus, Zürich, Vereinigung Zürcher Kunstfreunde. Oil on canvas, 163 x 231 cm

Tell us a Story, Papa Chagall

LAURENCE ANHOLT

Frances Lincoln
Children's Books

The twins were looking for their grandfather.

He wasn't
in the woodshed.

He wasn't with the goats.

He wasn't feeding the chickens.

"Hey, you two!" said Papa Chagall.
"I'm in here. I'm painting in my studio."

The studio was full
of wonderful pictures.
The twins saw...

a pink goat and a green man,

a weird cat on
a windowsill,

and a magical circus at night.

"Now then," said Papa Chagall,
"it's time to get back to work."

"Papa Chagall, Papa Chagall!
Tell us a story, Papa Chagall!"

"A story?" said Papa Chagall.
"Well, let's see... did I tell you
about when I was a little boy?

We lived in a topsy-turvy
town by a river. My mother
and father had nine children
and they were very poor.
But we were the happiest
family in the whole of Russia."

"You are always happy,
Papa Chagall!" said the twins.

"My mother had a tiny shop. She was always
giving me little treats... a hard-boiled egg
or a raw herring..."

"Yuck!" said the twins.

"Of course, she loved all her
children, but I think she liked
me best of all, because I had
curly hair and a twinkly smile."

"You still have curly hair,"
said the twins, "and a twinkly
smile too."

"We didn't have a TV or even a radio,
but in the evening all the family played music
and we told each other magical stories.

But there was one thing
I loved more than anything.
Can you guess what that was?"

"You loved painting!" said the twins.

"Exactly!" said Papa Chagall.
"I painted everything I saw,
and everything I dreamed of.

'These pictures are very peculiar,' said my father.
'Look, here is a purple cow with an umbrella.
Here is an old man flying over the rooftops!'

'Leave him alone,' said
my mother. 'His paintings
make me happy.'

'Let's settle this once and for all,'
said my father. 'There is a big
Art School in the town.
Let's ask the teacher if these
paintings are any good.'

Next day, my mother collected a pile of my paintings;
she took me by the hand and led me to the big Art School.
The teacher was a very serious man."

"Were you scared, Papa Chagall?" said the twins.

"I was so scared, I hid behind my mother's skirt.
The serious teacher stared at my paintings.
He looked at the purple cow and the flying man.
Then all of a sudden, he began to smile.
'These paintings are funny!' he said.

'But they are very, very good.
You must come to the Art School
and show everyone how
to paint purple cows.'

'How can he go to Art School?' said my mother.
'We don't have a single bean.'

'This boy is so talented, I will pay
for him to come to Art School,'
said the teacher.

And that's how I became a painter,"
said Papa Chagall.
"And I'm still painting now... at least I would be
if you two monkeys weren't distracting me!"

Then it was time for lunch.
They sat in the sunshine
and ate bread and cheese
and apples.

"Papa Chagall, Papa Chagall!
Tell us a story, Papa Chagall!"

"A story?" said Papa Chagall. "Well, let's see...
did I tell you how I met your granny?

One day I was coming home
and I saw a girl standing on
a bridge. Her name was Bella,
which means beautiful.

As soon as I saw her, I knew
that Bella was the one for me.

'I will come and see you on
your birthday,' she told me.

A few weeks later, I was painting in my room.

I had forgotten it was my birthday.

Then Bella knocked on the door.

She was carrying a bunch of flowers.

'Don't move!' I said. 'Stay where you are!'

'Why?' said Bella.

'Because I want to paint a picture of you holding the flowers.'

And that's how I met your granny.
Look, come inside. I'll show you the painting
I made. It's called The Birthday."

"Why are you flying?" said the twins.

"We are flying because we are so happy,"
said Papa Chagall.

"We got married and things got better still...
people began to like my funny paintings,
with the strange colours and the flying
animals. We went to live in Paris.

Then the best thing of all happened...
Can you guess what it was?"

"Bella had a baby!" shouted the twins.

"Yes, we had a baby girl
and we called her Ida.
We were the happiest family
in the whole of France."

"...And that was our mummy," said the twins.

At the end of the day,
Papa Chagall tucked them into bed.

"Papa Chagall, Papa Chagall!
Tell us a story, Papa Chagall!"

"A story?" said Papa Chagall.
"Well, let's see... did I tell you how we ran away?

When Ida was growing up, there was a war.
Everyone was frightened and everyone was sad.
Some bad people came – they hated me
and they did not like my paintings.
They made an exhibition of paintings by me
and my friends just so people could laugh at us."

"Then you weren't happy, were you, Papa Chagall?"

"No," said Papa Chagall. "I was not happy at all.
The bad people burnt houses and we had
to take a boat and run away to America.

Your mother was very brave.
She looked after us. She collected all my
paintings and put them safely in boxes.
All the way to America, she sat on the boxes
so that no one would touch them.

But I was scared for my family and friends.
I couldn't speak English and I became lonely.
I made lots of paintings about war. I was
the saddest painter in the whole of America."

Then the twins looked at Papa Chagall.
His twinkly smile had gone.
He didn't seem happy any more.

He kissed them good night
and put out the light.

In the night, the twins had scary dreams
about burning houses and frightened people.
They woke up crying.

"Papa Chagall, Papa Chagall!
Tell us a story, Papa Chagall!"

"A story?" said Papa Chagall. "Well, let's see...
did I tell you how I became rich and famous?

When the war was over, people were fed up
with being sad. They wanted something to
make them happy again. They looked at my
paintings with the purple cows and the flying
people and it made them smile.

People started buying my paintings for
a lot of money. I became a famous artist.
I met lots of other famous artists.
Soon I was a very rich man.

People asked me to make big coloured windows
and huge paintings for the theatre and the ballet
and they let your mother design the costumes.

I was the happiest painter in the world.
I made lots of pictures of people flying
high above the rooftops."

"I wish we could fly, Papa Chagall."

"Guess what?" said Papa Chagall.
"You can fly! In your imagination
and in your paintings and in your
dreams, you can fly as high as
you want."

Then the twins fell asleep
and they dreamed
happy dreams about flying
high in the sky
with Papa Chagall.

They didn't wake until the sun came through the curtains and the cockerel jumped up on the windowsill.

And where was Papa Chagall, with his curly hair and his twinkly eyes?

"I'm in here," said Papa Chagall. "I'm painting in my studio."

"Papa Chagall, Papa Chagall. Tell us a story, Papa Chagall..."

Chagall in Paris 1921

MARC CHAGALL (1887-1985) was born to Hasidic Jewish parents in Vitebsk, part of what used to be known as White Russia, now Belarus. His father was a poor herring merchant and his mother kept a tiny shop in a front room. Marc, with his curly hair and sparkling blue eyes, was the oldest of nine children.

He began drawing and painting at an early age, and the highly traditional teacher at the local art school was said to be so amazed at Chagall's use of colour and imagery, that he offered him free tuition. In spite of this, the poor student had to paint on old curtains and even his own shirts instead of canvas.

In 1909, the handsome young man fell in love with Bella Rosenfeld, who became his beloved wife and muse for more than 30 years. The birth of their daughter, Ida, seemed to complete their happiness. The Chagall family travelled to Paris, then Berlin, where Marc's extraordinary images of flying figures and scenes from Russian folklore were becoming popular. Unfortunately the works also attracted the attention of the Nazis,

who confiscated 59 of his canvasses, and in 1937 Chagall's work was included in the 'Degenerate Art' exhibition, which was designed to demolish Jewish art. As Chagall had become a French citizen, he did not wake up to the appalling dangers of anti-Semitism until Ida, newly married, begged her parents to flee to New York. She packed many of Chagall's greatest works into packing cases, which she guarded during the passage.

In spite of his growing reputation, Chagall was never happy in America and, although fluent in Russian, Yiddish and French, he refused to learn English. This was the lowest point of Chagall's life. As he heard about the suffering of Jews in Europe, his devoted wife, Bella, became ill and died in 1944.

Chagall finally settled in Vence in the south of France, with his second wife, Valentina Brodsky. Alongside his close neighbours, Matisse and Picasso, he became established as one of the greatest artists of the twentieth century.

Marc Chagall continued working until his 97th year. People still flock to galleries and museums all over the world to see the vibrant work of Marc Chagall – the man who told stories in paint.

MORE BOOKS IN THE ANHOLT'S ARTISTS SERIES

For over 20 years, the Anholt's Artists series has introduced readers to some of the world's most famous artists through the real children who knew them. Telling inspirational true stories and featuring reproductions of the artists' work, these titles bring art to life for children everywhere.

Anholt's Artists Activity Book
978-1-84507-911-6

Camille and the Sunflowers
978-0-71122-156-7

Cézanne and the Apple Boy
978-1-84780-604-8

Degas and the Little Dancer
978-0-71122-157-4

Leonardo and the Flying Boy
978-1-78171-515-4

Matisse: King of Colour
978-1-84507-632-0

Picasso and the Girl with a Ponytail
978-0-71121-177-3

The Magical Garden of Claude Monet
978-1-84507-136-3

"A great introduction to art . . . highly recommended."
— *The Observer*

Frances Lincoln titles are available from all good bookshops.
You can also buy books and find out more about your favourite titles,
authors and illustrators on our website: www.franceslincoln.com